MY FIRST BOOK OF

شکل‌ها و رنگ‌ها
SHAPES AND COLORS
IN FARSI

By Shereen Khundmiri

RŪXART
DIGITAL
DESIGNS

©RUXART 2020
All Rights Reserved.

This book belongs to:

_____

shapes

شکل‌ها

shekl-hâ

colors

رنگ‌ها
rang-hâ

circle

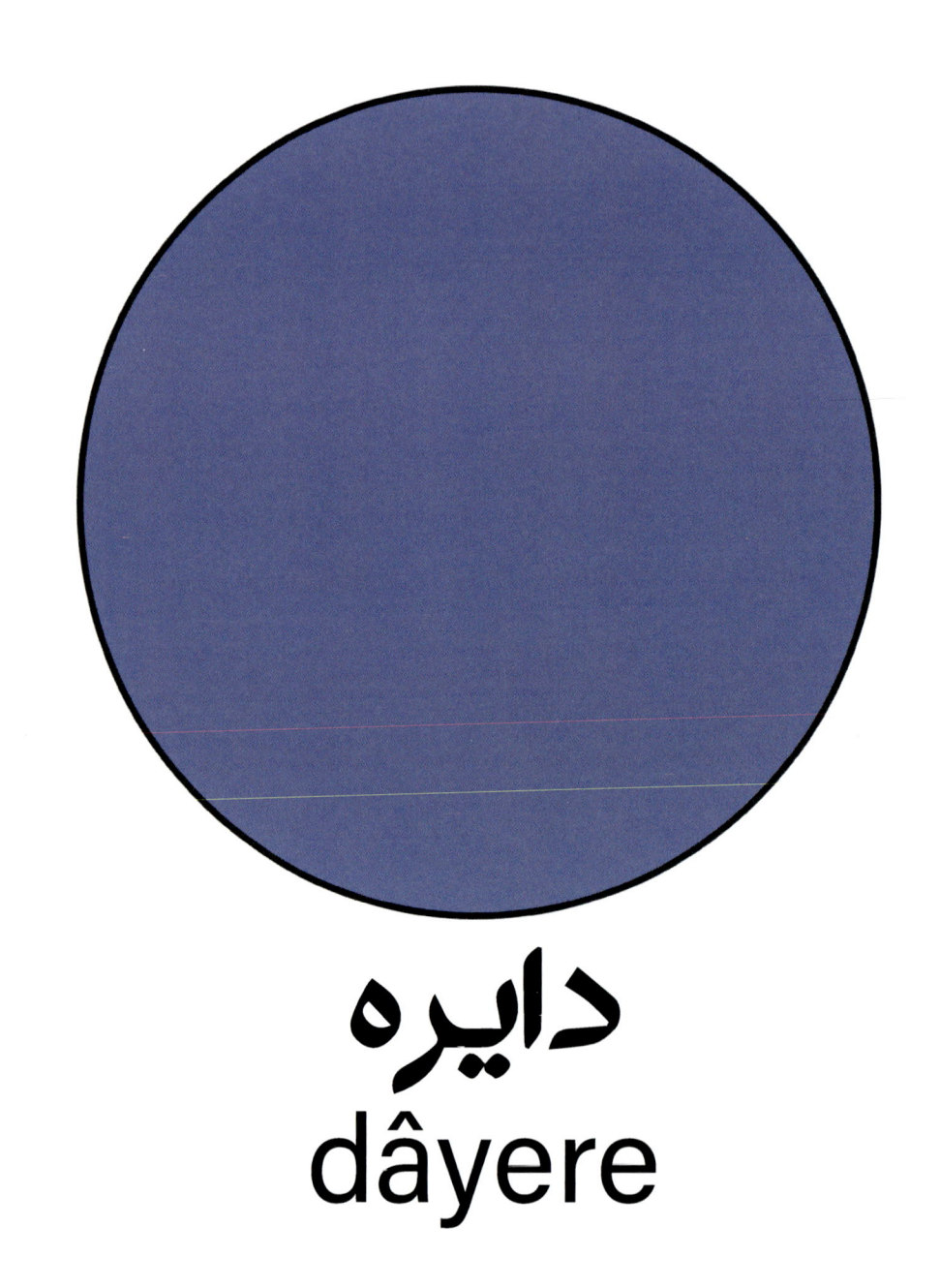

دایره
dâyere

این دایره آبی است

In dâyere aabi ast.
This circle is blue.

oval

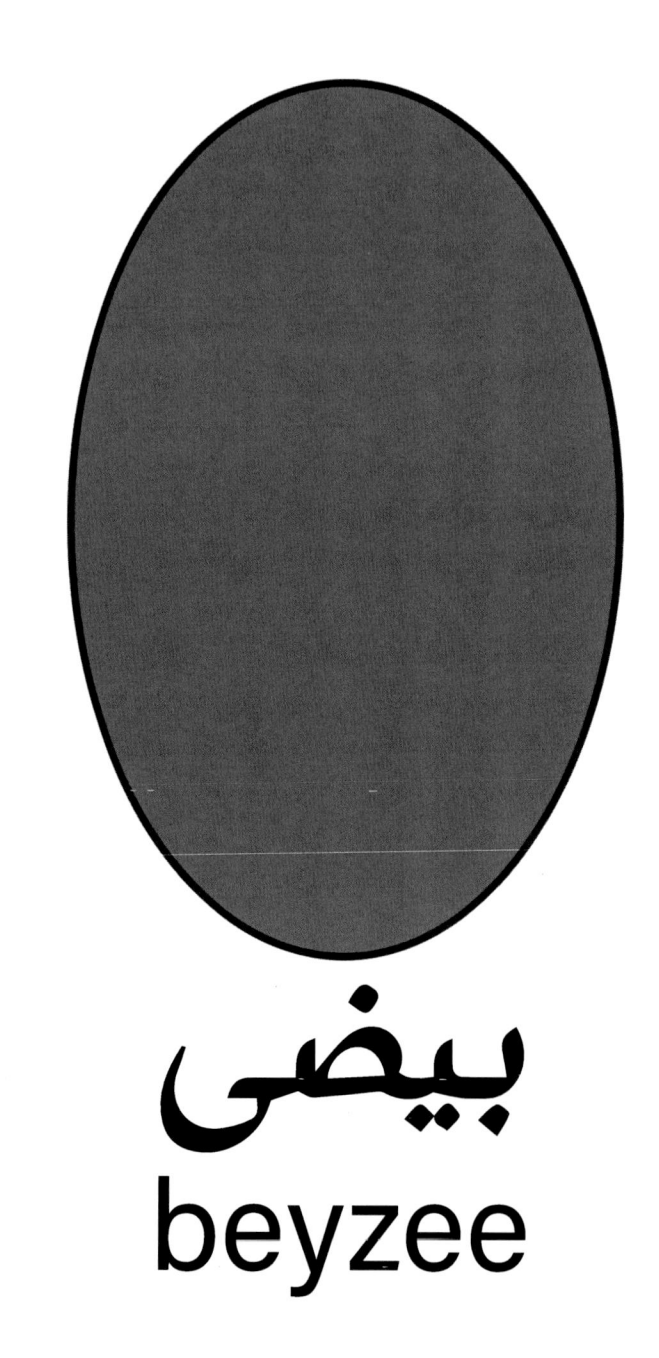

بيضى
beyzee

این بیضی خاکستری است

In beyzee khakestari ast.

This oval is gray.

square

مربع

morabba'

این مربع صورتی است

In morabba' soorati ast.
This square is pink.

rectangle

مستطيل
mostateel

این مستطیل قهوه‌ای است

In mostateel ghahveyi ast.

This rectangle is brown.

triangle

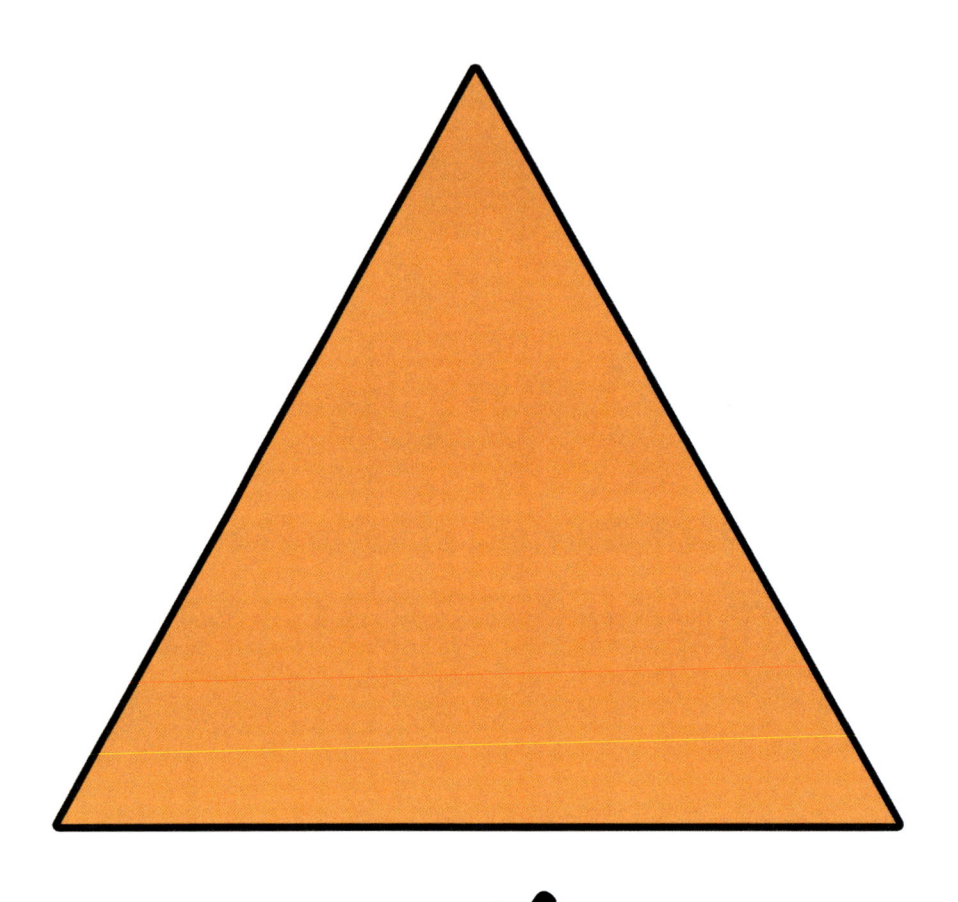

مثلث

mosallas

این مثلث نارنجی است

In mosallas nârenji ast.

This triangle is orange.

pentagon

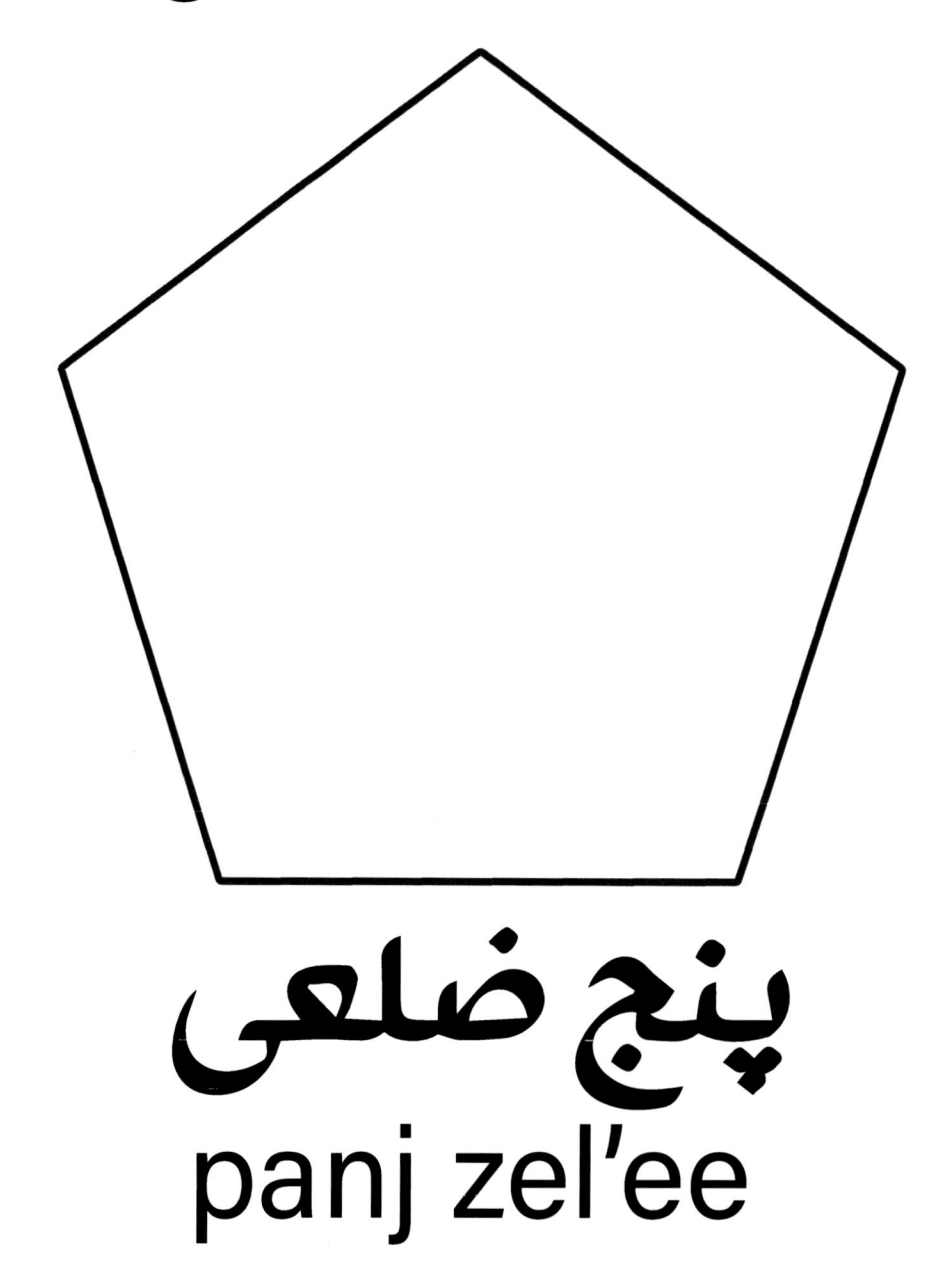

پنج ضلعی

panj zel'ee

این پنج ضلعی سفید است

In panj zel'ee sefeed ast.

This pentagon is white.

hexagon

ششش ضلعى

shesh zel'ee

این شش ضلعی سبز است

In shesh zel'ee sabz ast

This hexagon is green.

octagon

هشت ضلعی
hasht zel'ee

این هشت ضلعی سیاه است

In hasht zel'ee **seeyah** ast.
This octagon is **black**.

heart

قلب
ghalb

این قلب قرمز است

In ghalb ghermez ast.

This heart is red.

star

ستاره

setâreh

این ستاره زرد است

In setâreh zard ast.
This star is yellow.

diamond

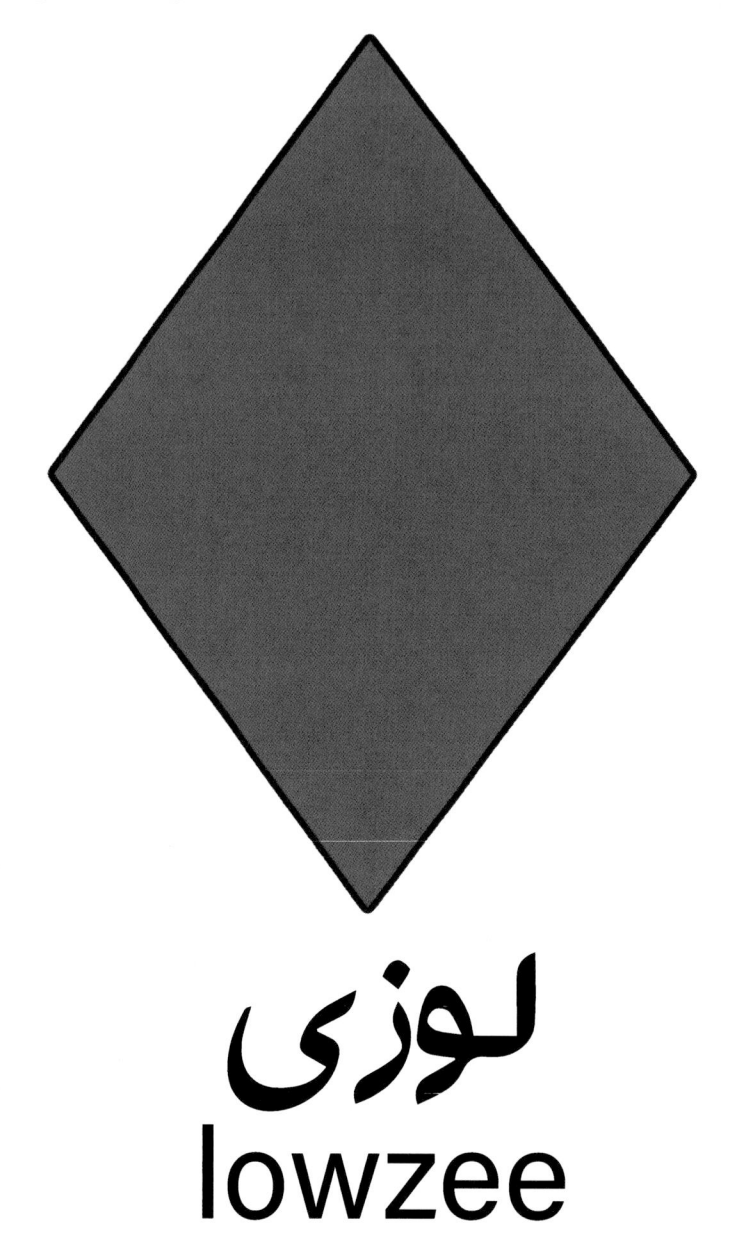

لوزى
lowzee

این لوزی بنفش است

In lowzee banafsh ast.
This diamond is purple.

RŪXART
DIGITAL
DESIGNS

Made in the USA
Las Vegas, NV
25 February 2024